I0625707

STORYLETS

A Collection
of First Chapters
to Inspire
New Authors

JAN SPURGEON

Self Published
NEW SMYRNA BEACH, FL

Jan Spurgeon/Self Published
Edited by Darren Spurgeon

Publisher's Note: This is a work of fiction. Names, characters, places, and incidents are a product of the author's imagination. Locales and public names are sometimes used for atmospheric purposes. Any resemblance to actual people, living or dead, or to businesses, companies, events, institutions, or locales is completely coincidental.

Storylets / Jan Spurgeon. — 1st ed.
ISBN 978-0-9892183-2-0

For all who may be inspired to finish what they started.

TABLE OF CONTENTS

INTRODUCTION

Are you ready to write but just can't seem to get started? Don't let that stop you. Here are some beginnings that may inspire you to keep going. These are all pretty short, so they shouldn't be intimidating.

Each is constructed as a first chapter of a longer work so that you have the character(s), setting, point of view, and suggestion of a plot line. In addition, for some you are given a premise for the story and for others, you will find possibilities, questions, and suggestions at the end. From there, your imagination can take over and go anywhere it takes you.

Most of the titles are topics, and a list of more topics has been placed at the end, in case you need more inspiration.

Browse through these ten storylets and see what happens!

ONE

INCIDENT AT THE POST OFFICE

Dust flew out the door ahead of Tyrone Baker as he swept the Post Office floor. It was a boring, mechanical action that allowed his mind to wander through the cosmic pool of musical knowledge in search of the elusive end to a refrain that had been haunting him for days.

This was no ordinary refrain, and if he could just latch on to the rest of it, he knew he'd have another big hit to his credit.

And maybe this time the royalties would give him the freedom to compose full time. This part-time job from five to midnight put bread on the table and paid his bills, but it sure cramped his creative urges.

Not until he started sweeping the dirt down the steps did he realize a discordant note had interrupted his brain waves.

Huddled by the metal railing attached to the edges of the steps was a pathetic figure whose body was shaking with wracking coughs. Hands flailed the air in futile attempts to wave the dust away.

"Get out of the way!" Tyrone growled. "I told you before not to hang around here. I could have you arrested for loitering. This is government property."

Rising slowly as the coughing subsided, the girl turned toward Tyrone and he could see that, though shapeless, her dress appeared to be clean underneath the thin layer of dust he had stirred up with his sweeping.

"Please," she implored, "could you just stop spreading dust for a moment so I can breathe?"

"Why should I do that? This is my job. For the past three days, I've chased you off these steps. You're nothing but a nuisance, and I should report you to the police."

The flash of fear in her eyes caused him to soften his voice, for he was not without compassion, having been close to desperation himself on more than one occasion. "What do you want?"

"I-I need a safe, dry place to spend the night, and I've managed to hide inside the Post Office for the last three nights."

At his look of outrage, she continued, "I thought it would be unlikely that someone would think to look for me here."

"If you need a place to stay, why not go to one of the shelters? They'll give you a bed and some food and even some clothes if you need them. You look like you could use both food and clothes." As he looked closer, he could tell that she was older than the teenager he had assumed she was.

"I can't go to a shelter. They're watching all the shelters and the parks, too. Please, just turn your back for a second and I'll disappear into my hiding place and you'll never know I was here."

Her eyes begged him, but he wasn't about to let his sympathy overrule his common sense. He could expect dire penalties if he got caught harboring a fugitive.

"No way! If you're in trouble, I want no part of it, so go find another place to hide," he advised her dismissively and continued sweeping the steps. However, he kept one eye on her as she stubbornly clung to the railing and watched him sweep around her feet.

When he finished the steps, he turned to find her in the same spot, still observing him.

"What's your name?" he asked abruptly.

"Jennifer," she whispered, and he didn't press her for a last name. He realized that even her first name might not be real.

Hoping she might reveal more information, he offered, "My name's Tyrone Baker," but she obviously wasn't ready to trust him.

"Who are 'they'? And why are they watching all the shelters and parks?"

When she remained silent, he stepped in front of her and glared until she lowered her gaze to her tightly-clasped hands. "I've watched you for days now, and you seem like a nice person. I just don't know what to do. I-I've got to tell someone, but I hate to involve you. It could be dangerous."

She slowly raised her head until her eyes met his. He could see that she was barely managing to prevent herself from falling in a crumpled heap on the steps. Her energy seemed to have drained completely away.

He dropped his broom, sat down on the step beside her, and gently folded her in his arms.

After several minutes, the young woman who called herself Jennifer sat up straight, took a deep breath, and began her story.

Creative Direction

- Who is Jennifer?
- Who are "they"?
- What has caused her to be so terrified?
- What kind of person is she when she isn't terrified?
- We already know that Tyrone is a musician/composer who is working at the Post Office in order to pay bills until he can write that elusive next big hit, so what does that tell you about his character?
- Why is the Post Office a good setting for this story?
- What are some possible ways that this story could develop?

TWO

ROOMMATES

Slamming the door behind her as usual, Morgan stepped into the living room, dropped her duffel bag on the floor, and continued into the room. She peeled off her jacket as she walked gracefully toward the silent figure huddled in a corner of the big sofa.

"Hey, Frannie, what's wrong?" She sank onto the sofa beside the unresponsive lump and reached out to touch a rounded shoulder. Still no movement. Francis was in her own world, but that didn't deter Morgan. Her eyes reflected concern over her friend's present withdrawal from their usual everyday activities.

"Fran? Come on, talk to me. I hope you haven't been sitting here since I left three hours ago."

Francis gradually stretched her voluptuous five-foot-six body into an upright position and raked trembling hands through disheveled auburn curls. If nothing else, her careless motions indicated distress, for she always took great care with her shoulder length hair, which she regarded as her only redeeming feature. In spite of her success as an actress, she always seemed surprised when heads turned to admire her natural grace and beauty.

"Hi, Morgan. How was dance class?" Fran's less-than-enthusiastic inquiry was a further indication of her depressed state of mind. Nevertheless, she looked questioningly at Morgan when she didn't get an immediate reply.

"It was fine, but I'm worried about you. Bruce didn't call, I suppose."

"You suppose right. He isn't going to call, Morgan. I told you that days ago. He's in love with someone else, and I'm never going to see him again," choked Francis as tears spilled from her eyes.

Morgan gathered her friend into her arms, wondering how in the world Fran had any more tears left after doing nothing else for almost a week. That jerk Bruce should be kicked into the next millennium, she thought again. Why Fran loved him so much was more than Morgan could understand. She hoped that when she fell in love, it would be with someone a lot nicer than Bruce, but she kept that thought to herself.

"I wish I were dead!" exclaimed Fran with more energy than she had shown since the day Bruce had broken their engagement.

"Don't say that!" returned Morgan. She wanted to add "He isn't worth it" but bit her tongue.

"Come in the kitchen with me while I cook dinner," she said instead. "You haven't eaten enough to keep a bird alive in the last few days, and I'm going to cook your favorite chicken and rice and a nice tossed salad."

"I—I couldn't eat a thing," Fran stammered and refused to move from the sofa when Morgan tried gently to pull her to her feet.

"I'll come and get you when it's ready," said Morgan as she headed for the kitchen, wishing she could think of some way to lift Fran from her deep depression.

The front door opened and closed and Morgan knew their friend and apartment mate had returned from work. She hoped John could help Fran see the world from her usual optimistic viewpoint again. Hearing two voices in the living room, Morgan began assembling ingredients for the meal that just might tempt Fran to eat at least a little.

Listening as she worked, Morgan could barely make out a few syllables now and then, though not enough to actually follow the low conversation. Still, John often established the connection that allowed Fran to pour out her troubles.

"Hi, Morgan," John greeted her from the doorway. "Shall we set the table for you?"

Morgan glanced up from pouring iced tea into three glasses and tried to hide her relief at the sight of Fran standing beside John. Apparently John's pleasant matter-of-fact manner had convinced Fran to come to the table, and maybe this tentative step would help restore Fran's vibrant personality.

Storylets by Jan Spurgeon

Smiling at her two friends as she followed them into the dining room, Morgan made a mental note to thank John privately for easing Fran out of the doldrums.

Creative Direction

- What time period could this be? Do you think it is in the 21st Century or earlier?
- How can you show the setting outside of this incident?
- You can guess that it is New York City, but maybe it's some other large city. What would the location have to do with their chances of landing an acting job?
- How do they support themselves in the meantime?
- You could choose one character and make him or her your main one with the others only part of the action.

THREE

THE MOVIE

What was this movie about? Hardly remembering how I came to be seated there, let alone what I was watching, I tried once again to suppress the shock of the last few hours. My frantic hope that a movie would take my mind off my dilemma now appeared futile. NOTHING could obliterate the horror of what I had witnessed this afternoon in the park.

Some vengeful fate had put me in the wrong place at precisely the time to change my life forever. *Stop thinking about it,* I told myself as I looked up at the screen and saw two characters locked in a passionate embrace.

O, brother, just what I need—a sweet, sentimental love story when my own life is in shreds and racing toward total destruction!

As I shifted restlessly in my seat, I glanced around the theater and realized someone was sitting next to me, but I didn't look directly at him. I barely registered the fact that it was a male, a rather large male.

I tried to concentrate once again on the screen, but my mind was in such turmoil that I had no idea what was going on. If I could manage to think this through, surely it would make some sort of sense.

As the plot moved relentlessly forward on the screen, I began to breathe a little more easily and my heartbeat was not racing quite so fast. Maybe I could finally begin to figure out what to do. Survival was my main goal.

First and foremost, I knew I had to eventually leave the theater. But how and when? He might be outside watching to see if I had ducked inside. I breathed deeply and prayed he hadn't seen me enter quickly in the midst of a group of people. How long would he wait? I had no idea how much longer the movie would last but knew I had to have a plan of action.

Should I get up and go the restroom and use my cell phone to call the police? They would never believe my story. Several other possibilities flitted disjointedly through my mind, but nothing crystalized as viable action.

"Excuse me," a deep voice murmured somewhere above and to the right of my head.

"It's okay." I turned my head to acknowledge his apology and instant terror froze me in mid-movement. I was looking directly into the cold, gray eyes I had last seen too close to me in the park—the very last thing I had seen before fleeing, terrified, from the body that was lying still and lifeless on the ground.

I began shaking uncontrollably, and the gray eyes faded into oblivion as I lost my tenuous grasp on consciousness.

Creative Direction

- Okay, now what? Do you think this is the beginning of the story, with flashbacks to let the reader know how we got to this point?
- Or is the story going on from here? If so, who is this frightening man? Did he kill the person whose body the narrator had seen in the park?
- How is this stranger connected to the body?
- What happens when the narrator regains consciousness?

FOUR

THE NOTE

As he swallowed the last bite of his hamburger, Richard glanced up and again caught the redhead staring at him. Although she quickly lowered her eyes, he had felt her green gaze more than once while he bolted down a quick lunch. *Do I know her?* he thought. *Surely I would remember such a stunning woman if I had met her.*

Maybe she wasn't actually looking at him but someone at another table behind him. Without turning all the way around, and in the process making a fool of himself, he couldn't be sure anyone was there. Neither could he see anyone looking at her as he casually glanced to either side.

Richard forced his attention back to the papers scattered on the table. He didn't have time to be distracted; it wouldn't do to be late for his two-o'clock appointment with a new client.. Still, he couldn't stop his eyes from homing in on her after only a few moments. Again, her eyes quickly shifted back to her plate.

Finishing the last page on which he was jotting notes in the margin, he felt the hairs on the back of his neck stand up and knew she must be near. It was only a fleeting sensation, however, as he looked up and watched her walk briskly by his table, her gaze fixed on the door ahead.

He sat perfectly still as she pushed open the door and vanished outside. Not in a long time had any woman captured his attention quite so completely—and he had no idea who she was. Her identity was a puzzle that would have to be solved if he wanted any peace of mind.

Shaking his head to clear it, he reached to pick up his scattered papers and noticed a small folded scrap of paper on top of the pile. It had not been there before, and his suddenly sluggish brain began to grasp the fact that only the woman could have put it there. She must have dropped it as she walked past.

He unfolded the paper and saw three words, printed in block letters: **TONIGHT 7:00 ANTONIO'S**. What did it mean? Was she meeting someone there? Was she asking him to meet her there? Why?

All sorts of scenarios flashed through his mind with the speed of light, none of them making much sense. Finally, he concluded that she must have dropped the note accidentally, since he still had no idea who she was, and she didn't look like the kind of woman who would try to pick up a stranger.

Suddenly, Richard snatched up his papers, stuffed them haphazardly into his briefcase, and slipped the scrap of paper into his pocket. He threw some bills onto the table and headed for the door.

Damn! He was going to be late for his appointment, but he knew with certainty where he would be at seven o'clock that night.

Creative Direction

- Your setting for Chapter Two will probably be ANTONIO'S at 7:00, soooo what happens? Is she expecting Richard? Why?
- Is she meeting someone else? If so, who? Man? Woman? Several people?
- Richard may speculate all he wants, but he has to resolve the mystery of that note, so you'll probably send him to the restaurant early because he can't get that redhead out of his mind. Don't you think he'll want to sit at a table in a quiet corner and observe the activities?
- Suppose she never acknowledges Richard? What does he do then?

FIVE

THE LETTER

Cordelia Wescott paced from the window to the desk and back again, an activity that had become second nature to her during the past week. Running her fingers through her auburn curls as she paced, she pondered for the millionth time what to do.

Thoughts bouncing around in her mind refused to coalesce into a solution, in spite of the fact that she had been over and over the problem constantly day and night until she thought she would scream.

In all of her thirty-two years, nothing had upset her equilibrium as thoroughly as this. Cori had a secret, a secret that had altered her life forever and threatened the future well-being of everyone she held most dear. She wished she could turn back the clock to the day before her earth-shattering discovery. She had to tell them, but she didn't know how.

Cori, as the oldest of four children, had always been the one "in charge", especially since she was five years older than her brother and eight years older than her twin sisters. The death of their father ten years ago had devastated them all, and their mother had turned over more and more of the family business matters to Cori, having given in to her grief until she had died almost six months ago.

It was in her role of family leader and administrator that Cori had been sitting at the old partner's desk in her father's study a week ago. Opening one of the drawers to extract a sheet of stationery, Cori had exerted a little too much pressure and the drawer had shot out of its tracks, dumping the contents onto the floor at her feet. As she reinserted the drawer and began to replace the contents, she noticed an envelope sticking out from the back of the drawer. Curious, she pulled it out and glanced at her mother's name and address and then the postmark.

Saigon, 1969—the year she was born. Wonder who could have been writing her mother from Saigon? Cori couldn't think of anyone her mother might have known who was in the service. Opening and reading the letter had shaken her to the very core of her being.

If she could believe her eyes, Cori's whole life had been a lie. The father she had always adored was not her father; instead, it was someone named Kyle Landry, whoever that might be.

As he said in the letter, this Landry person was very much in love with Cori's mother. He was thrilled that she was pregnant with his child, said he could hardly wait to come home and marry her. Why didn't he? And why had Cori's mother never told her?

She had to find some answers. But first, she had to break the news to her brother and sisters—no, her half-brother and half-sisters.

So many questions bombarded her that Cori felt dizzy from the strain of trying to sort everything out. Had Owen Wescott adopted her? Neither he nor her mother had ever mentioned it, and they had always seemed so open with her that it would have been natural for them to let her know from the beginning.

They had told her they had been married more than a year before she had been conceived. Come to think of it, though, she had never actually seen a marriage certificate. There was none in the safe deposit box where all the important papers had been kept.

Did she now have a legal right to her inheritance? She hadn't looked at her birth certificate in years, but she was sure that Owen Wescott's name was on it. Her father and, later, her mother had taken care of most of the family legalities.

She had no choice now but to start delving into everything and she wondered how her findings would change her relationship with her siblings, for she loved them with all her heart. What a mess!

Finally, she stopped her pacing and lectured herself sternly, *Cori Wescott, or whoever you are, you do not have to do this alone! You have a brother and two sisters who love you as much as you love them, even if they are your half-brother and half-sisters.*

Having finally made the decision for action, Cori lifted the phone and called all three siblings, telling them only that they needed to meet to discuss family business. She didn't have the heart to inform them that all of their lives could be changed forever, but they had to see the letter. Then, as always before in their closely-connected lives, they would work it out together.

Tomorrow would be soon enough to call the family attorney and begin to uncover the truth that lay buried somewhere in the past.

Creative Direction

- Upon discovering an old letter in a family des, many people would just toss it in the trash, but not our character. This letter contains a life-changing message!
- What will she do with the shocking information and how will it affect others?

SIX

THE SECRET

The secret was always with her. Like a cancer, its tentacles spread insidiously throughout her mind and body, consuming her every thought and action. Sleeping or waking, she couldn't shake free of its control.

Ever the quintessential secretary, Carol Baker always arrived before her boss, made a pot of coffee, and greeted co-workers cheerfully while checking messages and organizing her boss's day. Though now she did these things mechanically, her heart was in turmoil. What should she do? That question was always with her.

She had managed his professional life like a well-oiled machine since he hired her twenty-five years ago next month. Her husband, her three children, and her church and community activities all were managed with the same efficiency, sense of humor, and complete devotion. She loved her family and friends unreservedly and respected and admired her boss.

"Have you got a cold?" More than one person had asked lately, noticing the dark circles under her eyes. She always managed to reassure the well-wishers that she would be fine when she had a chance to rest. Blithely, they took for granted that Carol would soon be her old cheerful self again.

"Carol, why don't you make an appointment with Doctor Blalock?" her husband Jake had asked again that morning. "You hardly ate any breakfast, and you can't afford to lose any more weight."

"I'm okay, just have a lot on my mind," she assured him. But, after twenty-eight years of marriage and raising three children together, Jake wasn't buying it. Something serious was wrong.

Knowing and loving her so well, though, he didn't press her for details; she would confide in him when she was ready. It wasn't likely that some life-threatening condition had her in its clutches, as her yearly checkup had resulted in a clean bill of health.

He just wished that she would confide in him soon, as it made him feel helpless to watch his usually happy wife drag herself through each day. Thank goodness the children—one married and living in California and the other two in college—were not around to see their mother on a day-to-day basis!

Carol sighed as she sat at her desk and thought about how she had liked and respected her boss of twenty-five years and how everything had changed almost three months ago. On that one ordinary day, in only a few stunning moments of time, her whole life shattered into a million pieces.

And yet, no one else knew, or even suspected, especially her boss. What would happen if she told him? Certainly nothing would ever be the same again, and plans for a well-deserved retirement would disappear in a flash.

Should she do what she knew was right?

Creative Direction

- What do you think Carol's secret is? Obviously, you need to decide before you can go forward with the story.
- *Chapter One* reveals a lot about Carol and how the secret has affected all aspects of her life, including plans for her upcoming retirement.
- Will she face her boss with her knowledge, or will she continue to suffer in silence?
- Deciding what the secret is and what Carol does about it is your challenge.

SEVEN

DINNER AND DISASTER

Jenny decided that this hot, muggy day would have to go down in her personal history as one of the worst on record since she went into partnership with Angelica about a year ago.

Not only had the ancient air conditioner chosen this day to develop a glitch, but minor disasters had begun before the restaurant opened at ten, when two of the regular waitresses had called in with the flu. Replacements had not yet arrived.

Pressed into waitressing, Jenny went from table to table, trying valiantly to maintain her sunny smile. She loved this business, which was finally beginning to show a small profit. A few more days like today, though, and it was anybody's guess as to how long they could keep the doors open.

Jenny, a fifty-two-year-old widow, had only a high school education and very little training other than the skills she had developed as a wife and mother. The mere contemplation of failure gave her the shivers.

Two young women came and stood quietly laughing and chatting until Angelica seated them at a small table in the back. Jenny hurried over, greeted them with a smile, and took their orders. Thank goodness the chef was in a good mood—at least that was a plus on this hectic day.

Returning to the table with their drinks, Jenny looked up to see Stewart Johnson standing just inside the front door. Her heart performed a double flip and she suppressed a groan. Why now? she wondered.

She had not seen or heard from Stewart since she had called off their affair more than two years ago. It had not been a pleasant scene, for they had been friends as well as lovers. Jenny had not wanted to make their relationship permanent and Stewart had. Oh, well, she couldn't ignore him; after all, he was a customer.

"Hello, Stewart." Jenny smiled tentatively at the shocked expression on Stewart's face.

"What are you doing here?" exclaimed Stewart. He didn't look at all happy to see her and she wouldn't have been surprised if he had turned around and walked back out the door.

"I'm Angelica's business partner. Are you expecting someone to join you for lunch? We have one table left."

"That's fine," he muttered, looked around distractedly, and followed her to the table adjacent to the two attractive young women. She handed him a menu and hurried to the kitchen to see if the previous orders were ready.

When she returned with the food, both young ladies were standing beside their chairs, looking at the ceiling , from which a steady stream of water was pouring onto their table. Oh, no! The air conditioner was on overload. No sooner had the thought registered than Stewart jumped up from his chair, brushing water from his hair.

Frantically, Jenny looked around to see where she could put the three customers. She spotted a large round table at which were seated only two people, an attractive older woman and a beautiful young woman who had the same expensively-groomed appearance.

"Pardon me," said Jenny. "The air conditioner is leaking over those two tables and I wondered if these customers could sit here until we can rearrange their tables."

A look almost of relief passed briefly between the two before the older woman nodded regally in acquiescence. Thank heavens for small blessings, thought Jenny as she transferred food and tableware to the big table amid awkward silence.

"Hi, I'm Alison Young and this is my friend Sandi Collins," offered the taller of the two women. "I'm an assistant district attorney and Sandi is an attorney with Becker, Collins, and Draper. We try to have lunch together every week or so just to keep in touch."

"We've been friends forever, but our schedules are both so full that we have to have a standing appointment just to keep up with each other." Sandi smiled as she looked around at the others, inviting them to introduce themselves.

"I'm Risa Granger and this is my mother, Marilyn," chirped the youngest of the group, looking relieved to have company. Her mother's smile was slightly strained as she acknowledged the introduction.

Almost as an afterthought, Stewart raised his head and added, "And I'm Stewart Johnson. I—"

At that instant, his eyes encountered wide, vaguely-familiar blue eyes across the table, eyes that reflected the same shock he felt all the way down to his toes. It couldn't be! But it was!

"Marilyn Jameson? Is it really you?"

"Stewart, I—" whispered Marilyn, her hands gripping the edge of the table. The room began spinning and she took several deep breaths as she prayed not to faint. Stewart, her first love, her college sweetheart, the man she would have married if she hadn't met Edward thirty-five years ago.

How extraordinary to be sitting here discussing her daughter's coming wedding and to suddenly be faced with Stewart, the man she *should* have married. Life is funny, she thought as blackness engulfed her and she sank slowly and gracefully to the floor.

Creative Direction

One interesting way to "juice up" your creativity is to go into a restaurant in which you know no one and imagine that some of the people are linked together, whether they know it or not. You can choose your characters by their appearance and actions (without being obvious, of course!). Decide what their connection(s) could be and you have what you need to develop a story!

EIGHT

A CONTEST OF WILLS

"I don't need anyone to protect me," she said. Tucking a strand of honey-blonde hair behind one ear, Jeanine Hoffman gathered her purse and started to rise from the uncomfortable straight-backed chair in which she had been perched for more than an hour.

"I need to get back to my office or I'll be late for my two o'clock appointment."

"Wait, Miss Hoffman. I can't make it any plainer—we still don't know who threatened you, but the man did sound like he meant business. After listening to the answering machine message again, I'd feel better if you'd let me assign someone to keep an eye on you. One of the female officers could move in with you, go with you to the office, or wherever. She could pose as a friend visiting from out of town—"

"Absolutely not!" exclaimed Jeanine. "I value my privacy and, besides that, the cases I handle are very sensitive. Most of the women I represent have barely escaped alive, not to mention the children whose trauma is immeasurable. I won't have someone hanging around, intimidating my clients."

Lieutenant Jared McCloud sighed with frustration. Once again, he managed to control his rising temper as he mentally looked for another way to convince her that her life really was in danger.

This was one stubborn woman, but he knew he couldn't force her to accept police protection. He also knew she wasn't taking the situation as seriously as he was; something about that menacing voice was vaguely familiar to him.

He couldn't place it, although his memory for faces and voices was legendary among his long-time colleagues. He just hoped he could recall where and when he had heard that voice before it was too late.

"All right," he capitulated. "Have it your way...for now...but stay alert, and don't do anything foolish." He stood and held the door as she glided gracefully out of his office. More than one admiring male gaze followed her progress to the outside door.

"Henderson!" He motioned to an attractive female officer seated at a nearby desk and waved her into his office, shutting the door and rounding his cluttered desk to drop wearily into his chair.

"Here's what I want you to do," he ordered, and explained the situation. After several pertinent questions, she nodded and left the office.

That's the best I can do, he thought, *until she agrees to protective custody...or...until something else happens.*

Now that his office was completely quiet and he could focus his attention once again on that voice, he punched the play button on the tape recorder and leaned back in his chair.

Creative Direction

- What can happen when you have two strong-willed characters who don't agree on something and neither is willing to compromise?
- Do you think one is right and the other is wrong?
- This *Chapter One* indicates danger as well as more personality clashes ahead.
- You should determine how you want the story to end before you plot the series of events that will lead to that end.

NINE

A STRANGE CASE

"What happened?" queried Zack. He ignored the stars spinning around in his head and carefully surveyed what looked to be an institutional room of some sort.

"Shhh...you'll be all right," crooned a pleasant voice as a warm, soft hand touched his arm and gently pushed him back down.

He looked up into concerned brown eyes and, upon further visual exploration, realized they belonged to a nurse who was standing very close to the bed on which he lay.

As he opened his mouth to repeat his question, he was startled by a giggle. Standing just inside the door was a young woman with her eyes as round as saucers and both hands pressed firmly over her mouth, trying unsuccessfully to contain more giggles.

"Who the hell is she?" he demanded, glaring at the woman and struggling to sit up. "What's so funny?"

"Angie, go back to your room," gently ordered the nurse, reaching to push Zack down again. She was unprepared for his sudden burst of strength and nearly lost her balance when he swung his arm into her side.

"I've had enough of this! I want to know where I am and what's going on!" His voice had gained volume until he was shouting the last phrase.

"You're in Sleepy Rest Sanitarium," said a stern, no-nonsense voice from the vicinity of the doorway.

Zack looked up into the face of a tall, blue-eyed, gray-haired man in a white lab coat. "I'm Dr. Halsey, by the way, and I'll take over now, Nurse McKensie."

Nurse McKensie smiled, patted Zack on the shoulder, and headed for the door, herding the young woman ahead of her as she went out and shut the door softly behind her.

"What's going on? Why am I here? How did I get here? Answer me, Doc!" growled Zack as he gripped the man by both shoulders and shook him firmly.

"Hold on, now, let's not get excited," cautioned the doctor. "You're not in any condition to be rambunctious, young man."

Just as he opened his mouth to again demand some answers, Zack noticed the door slowly swinging inward. A giggle followed and two big brown eyes peeked around the edge.

"There she is again!" yelled Zack. "Who is she and what is she doing here?"

"My, you certainly have a lot of questions, Mr. Johnson," drawled the doctor as he sat in a chair close by the bed. "Which one do you want answered first?"

"First, I want that girl out of here," ordered Zack, pointing at the girl who was inching closer to the bed.

"She's just interested in any new patient. She has been here most of her life and we let her have the run of the place. She's harmless, aren't you, Angie?" He smiled at her and she nodded and giggled again. Suddenly, she turned and ran out of the room, slamming the door in her haste.

"Now, tell me what's going on." Zack glared at the doctor, who looked as if he had settled in for a long chat.

"You were admitted last night by your wife and—"

"Wife!" exclaimed Zack. "I don't have a wife!"

"Of course you don't. It's all been cleared up. That's what I came to tell you. Some woman found you wandering the street close by, babbling incoherently about killing someone, so she dragged you in here and told the receptionist to call the police. "In all the excitement, the receptionist thought the woman was your wife and called me. I gave you a shot to calm you down and you've been sleeping for almost twenty-four hours. "Meanwhile, the police have not found the murderer. Neither did they find the woman who brought you in and probably saved your life. Do you remember what happened before she found you?"

"No, I don't, and how do you know my name?"

"We found a wallet in your pocket and assumed it was yours. Your picture's on your driver's license. Also in your pocket was your police identification, which led me to contact your precinct captain. Are you sure you don't remember what happened?"

"I—"

Suddenly the door burst open and a short, chubby man in a rumpled suit hurried in. He stopped at the sight of Zack half-sitting on the bed and said, "I came as soon as I heard. Are you all right?"

"Who are you?" asked Zack, a puzzled frown wrinkling his weary face.

"You don't know who I am? I'm your partner, Bill Wright." He turned his worried countenance toward the doctor and whispered, "What's wrong with him?"

"Don't talk about me as if I'm not here," grumbled Zack.

"I'm Doctor Halsey," offered the doctor, "and I was just explaining to Mr. Johnson how he came to be here.

"Now that you have arrived, I'll release him into your care with my recommendation that he see a medical doctor and a psychiatrist to deal with his injuries and the amnesia. The paper work is all done."

"Thanks, Doc. I'll take it from here," said Bill.

"Good-bye, gentlemen." Wearily, Doctor Halsey trudged out the door.

"Are you ready to go, Zack?" As Bill started toward the door, with Zack stumbling dazedly behind him, his voice floated back from the hallway. "Boy, have you had an adventure today! I can hardly wait 'til the Captain hears about this latest case."

I can't wait either, thought Zack as he tried to hurry and catch up.

Creative Direction

- What could have happened to Zack before this Chapter One began?
- Now that he seems to have lost his memory, how can you move the story forward?
- Do you think he committed murder? Or did he witness one? Or maybe he was mugged?
- You have a lot of possibilities to work out before you can determine the outcome.

Storylets by Jan Spurgeon

- Do you think Zack has the gumption to figure out the who, what, when, where, why, and how in spite of his amnesia?
- He does have a trusty sidekick who may or may not know something!!!

TEN

THE LEGACY

Jamie Connor drove the rental car up the long drive and stopped. Stepping out, she stretched her cramped muscles and looked around, finally gazing in awe at the huge Victorian house that sat, like a giant mother hen, atop the slight knoll. *Rather like a queen wearing a crown of glorious jewels*, she thought, as the sun momentarily gilded the fiery leaves of the ancient oaks and maples surrounding the house.

Never having been to the mountains of North Carolina, Jamie was unprepared for the breathtaking sights that filled her senses on the drive here. All the way from the airport in Ashville through the rolling foothills, Jamie had marveled at the myriad of vibrant golds, reds, and browns that gilded the countryside, contrasting and enhancing the evergreens. And she had always thought New York was spectacular in the Fall!

She didn't need this complication in her life now, of all times. Known to her associates as J.P. Connor, Jamie had worked six long years to accomplish her goal of becoming a junior partner in a prestigious Manhattan law firm by the time she was thirty-five. She had made it three years before her self-imposed deadline and was singularly proud of her achievement, which represented eighty-hour work weeks and untold sleepless nights. But she loved it!

A city girl born and bred, Jamie loved the fast-paced drama of her chosen profession as well as the wonderful city in which she had spent most of her life. Not happy about this interruption to her well-ordered though hectic existence, she had briefly contemplated ignoring the whole thing, but curiosity had won out in the end and here she was, a stranger in a strange land, so to speak.

Whatever could her father's eccentric aunt have been thinking to leave this monstrosity to Jamie, who had never even met the old lady? No one could have been more surprised than she when the large envelope had arrived last week from Aunt Hettie's attorney.

An immediate phone call to her dad had failed to shed any light on this unusual bequest or on the stipulation that Jamie must live in the house for three months before she could sell it.

"You should go, Jamie," her dad had advised. "Although you never met her, she knew all about you, as your mother and I talked to her regularly. She was always interested in what you were doing."

"But, Dad," Jamie had insisted, "I really don't have three months to spare"

"Aunt Hettie never did anything without a reason," replied Dad, and Jamie reluctantly started working out the details.

Obviously, the ninety-one-year-old lady had cared nothing about what it would do to Jamie's career, job security, lifestyle, or anything else except to ensure that her own wishes, whatever they were, were carried out.

Gritting her teeth once again at such a ridiculous situation, Jamie sighed, reached into the large manilla envelope on the front seat, and extracted a ring of keys.

Striding up the winding brick walkway and onto the wraparound porch, Jamie inserted the ancient key clearly labeled "front door" into the lock, opened the door, and stepped inside.

Momentarily stunned, Jamie dizzily wondered if she had entered a time warp. The furnishings, the knick knacks, even the atmosphere were early twentieth century, especially the dark furniture, the heavily varnished wood floors and wainscoting, and the dark colors of the walls.

Futilely, she strained to see into the far reaches of the large room in which she was standing, but even the bright afternoon sunlight failed to penetrate the shadows. Feeling her way along the wall beside her, she finally found a light switch and flipped it on.

The chandelier above her winked on, spreading a pattern of fractured light from the faceted crystals dangling high above her head. Its feeble effort did little to dispel the gloom of what seemed to be a large central hall.

Various doors were opened into rooms to the left, right, and directly in front of her. Wide stairs rose to a landing topped by a huge stained glass window and branched off to right and left, where Jamie could see other doors leading, she presumed to the bedrooms.

Overwhelmed by the sheer size of the house, almost ready to hyperventilate, Jamie whirled around to open the front door for some fresh air. And stopped dead in her tracks! There on the other side of the oval etched-glass door panel was the hulking form of a man, peering in at her. As her heart kicked into overdrive, she looked wildly around. Trapped! She didn't even know where the back door was.

Growing and working in Manhattan had honed her senses to a fine edge. She had two black belt degrees in the martial arts and the confidence to go with them. However, nothing had prepared her for the sight of such a large man just on the other side of a flimsy glass door. And who knew how many ghosts of spirits past might be gathered in these dark rooms, just waiting to pounce.

A light knock sounded on the door and the handle turned. Damn! She hadn't even thought to lock it, she'd been so overwhelmed with the atmosphere. What to do now? Run, or stand firm and face whatever was to come?

Taking a deep breath, two steps backwards for leverage, and assuming a defensive stance, she waited as the door swung slowly open. Show no fear— but be ready to kick butt! Her karate instructor's words gave her the courage to stand tall—all five feet two of her.

"Who are you? What are you doing here?" She demanded as he was halfway into the hall.

"I could ask you the same question. And how did you get in here?" He towered over her, pinning her to the spot with the most intense blue eyes she had ever seen. A nose that looked to have been broken at some time, firm, full lips, and dark blond hair that just touched the collar of the plaid shirt he wore with snug-fitting jeans were details that flitted like lightning through Jamie's fear-sharpened mind.

His height topped six feet and the muscles in his chest, arms, and thighs were impressive. But he was no bigger than one of her fellow black belt instructors whom she had downed more than once. Could she take him?

With the adrenaline that was coursing through her veins and the element of surprise, she thought it was worth a try if he reached for her.

"I asked you a question," he growled.

Jamie cut her eyes toward one of the doors on her right and, when he glanced in that direction, she pounced. He landed on his back on the floor, with her foot on his throat, cutting off his air supply. As his eyes began to roll back in his head, she eased her foot up to give him room to breathe, grabbed a heavy brass candlestick from a nearby table, and stood ready to bash him, her heart still pumping so fast she was almost lightheaded herself.

Without looking behind her, she calculated the distance to the door. Always look for an escape route—a rule that had been pounded into her from early childhood. She had no means of getting help; her phone was in the car, and there were no other houses close by, so screaming wouldn't help. She'd have to bash him and then run to the car. But first, she wanted to know who he was and what he was doing in *her* house.

Rubbing his throat with one hand, he used the other to lever himself to a sitting position, his eyes never leaving Jamie as she stood ready with the candlestick.

"What the Sam Hill—? Put that thing away. You've already done enough damage. I may never be able to talk normally again," he rasped, continuing to gently rub his throat.

"Not until you tell me who you are and what you're doing in my house!" she exclaimed, still standing over him with the candlestick raised and her entire body ready for defense.

Suddenly his face relaxed into a smile, which took Jamie's breath away. Wow! Her knees weakened in response. Watch out, advised a warning voice in her befuddled brain. With a smile like that, he could subdue whole nations of people.

"Are you by any chance J.P. Connor?"

"Yes. Not that it's any of your business."

"Ah, but it is my business. I'm Josh Nelson, Hettie's attorney. May I get up now?" He was already rising to his feet before she belatedly nodded and reached to replace the candlestick.

"I'd offer to shake hands, but I'm not too fond of landing on my back on hard surfaces," he informed her wryly.

"I apologize, but I had no idea who you were or what you were doing here," murmured Jamie as she looked up, way up, into those incredible blue eyes, feeling heat rising up her neck and into her cheeks. *What's wrong with me? I haven't blushed since I was fourteen,* she thought distractedly.

"Apology accepted. You never contacted me, so I wasn't expecting anyone." His expression clearly indicated that he thought she should have informed him of her plans instead of just showing up unannounced.

"It took a lot of rearranging to clear my calendar and I never thought of letting anyone other than my family know I was coming."

"So you're going to honor the will and stay the three months?"

"I guess I don't have any choice, although I *will* be handling several cases from here. I brought my computer, fax, cell phone, and case files, and I'll be in frequent touch with my partners," she said as she began to pace, already lost in mentally organizing her coming days.

"Well, I'll let you get on with settling in. If there's something you need, call my office. And slow down. This is Murrayville, not Manhattan. We don't go in for all that scurrying around. Relax and enjoy life...you'll live longer," he advised, smiling. He walked out the door, closing it softly behind him.

Whew! That smile would melt the entire North Pole, thought Jamie. She began to speculate that her three months' exile in this small town might not be so bad after all.

Creative Direction

Many people fantasize about receiving a legacy; probably the most common fantasy involves a lot of money or some other kind of "treasure". In reality, however, a legacy doesn't always fit the fantasy and can be quite a surprise and inconvenience to the recipient!

TOPICS AND TITLES FOR INSPIRATION

Setting

These topics would seem to suggest an emphasis on the element of setting as the basis for the story. However, you need well-developed characters, suitable dialog, and a clear point of view to carry the plot.

- Feathers on the Wind
- Moonbeams and Magic
- Spring Rain
- Clock Ticking
- Midnight Madness
- The Eagle Soars
- Reunion
- Rocks
- The Moon is Blue
- A Single Rose
- A Hammer
- Falling Leaves
- The ATM Machine

Character Development

These topics suggest emphasis on character development as the main element of the story, but don't forget the setting, dialog, and point of view as you develop your plot.

- Where the Rainbow Ends
- What Went Wrong
- 'Cat Fight'
- Lies and Legalities
- Operation Stargazer
- Blood Brothers
- Nobody Knows
- Best-Laid Plans
- No Pressure, No Diamonds
- A Tangled Web of Lies
- Hot Stuff

Point of View

Point of view is often difficult to maintain once you get caught up in the story, for most stories are written in third person point of view (he slammed the door, etc.). However, first person POV can be very effective in pulling the reader into the story ("Call me Ishmael", or I could feel the cold breath of the killer as he tried to choke me, etc.). Second person POV is less popular, though also effective with the right kind of story (you need to do something about the situation, etc.).

- My Turn Now
- Plate Glass Window
- Spring Fever
- Love Your Enemies
- The Eyes of the Blind
- Nobody's Business But Mine
- Unforgiven
- Have You Heard?
- The Searchers
- Home Shopping

ABOUT THE AUTHOR

Jan Spurgeon is a former high school English teacher who likes to write and to teach writing. With many years of teaching Creative Writing and Journalism to high school students, she also taught adult classes in writing for publication.

Other Books By This Author

Jan has published a workbook for adults entitled *GRAMMAR GREMLINS: A Little Blue Book Of Review*, available from Amazon.com.

ABOUT THIS BOOK

Writers, whether just starting out, or experienced, or somewhere between–here's a chance to brainstorm!

STORYLETS are beginnings of ideas, infants whose growth can result in short stories, novels, etc. Ideas come from everywhere–nothing new, just different uses and approaches. Some of these were born in brainstorming sessions in monthly writers' groups. Others were created to serve as models for point of view, character development, use of dialog, and other aspects of good writing. Obviously, each is intended to begin a longer work in the same style and with components already in place. Take a look inside–you'll probably find just what you need to inspire you to start writing!

Visit Storylets.com for more inspiration.